Henry!

WRITTEN BY

Mary Evanson
Bleckwehl

ILLUSTRATED BY

Brian Barber

you're hungry AGAIN?

To Luciana

This Book Belongs to _Luciana Megan D._

Mary Blackwehl

To my own three children—Nicole, Mike
and Tyler—who seemed to be hungry a lot.

—M.B.

To my mom and dad, who paid the grocery
bills while I was growing up.

—B.B.

ISBN 13: 978-1-59298-545-6

Library of Congress Catalog Number: 2012914132

Printed in the United States of America

Third Printing: 2018

21 20 19 18   6 5 4 3

Cover and interior design by Brian Barber

Edited by Jennifer C. Manion

Mary Bleckwehl photo by Tricia Little

Beaver's Pond Press, Inc.
7108 Ohms Lane
Edina, MN 55439-2129
(952) 829-8818
www.BeaversPondPress.com

To order, visit www.ItascaBooks.com or call 1-800-901-3480. Reseller discounts available.
For more information visit www.marybleckwehl.com

Can you hear it?

Sometimes it whispers to me.

But mostly it bellows,

Henry! you're hungry AGAIN!

It starts in the morning.

Mom says I'm old enough
to fix my own breakfast.

So I do!

Dad says coffee is enough. But I prefer something that tastes better than burnt rubber tires.

My baby brother, Ryan, has it easy.

And then there's my sister, the queen of polka-dot underwear and all other things in the Sister Queendom.

"Isabela, aren't you going to eat breakfast?" I ask.

All queeny-like, she announces, "Why, my lowly servant, the Royal Highness Isabela is taking her breakfast in bed."

Oh boy . . .

"Perchance would my peasant brother like some?"

I just love a sharing sister, I mean . . . queen.

I go to school. At nine o'clock it's SEAR time.
Teacher says SEAR is a secret code for "Stop Everything
And Read." I wish it were code for "Start **Eating** And Read."

I choose a book called *The Very Hungry Caterpillar*.

They say books give you ideas …

Finally, it's snack time. I'm feeling a little shaky, so I wolf down Queen Isabela's royal licorice. Her Highness's jawbreakers are pretty good, too—until Parker Hendricksen comes over.

"You know what will happen if you eat that junk all the time? Your teeth will rot and fall out, and instead of getting money from the tooth fairy, you'll have to get pretend teeth like my great-grandpa."

"Who says?"

"Sophie."

Now I'm a bit worried. Sophie is Parker's sister, AND she's the smartest kid in school.

At math time, I feel tired and hungry AGAIN. Teacher hands out twenty red candies and two paper cups to each kid.

"Students, I want you to put the candies in your two cups so there is the same amount in each cup."

She waits.

"Now class, how many red candies do you have in each cup?"

"Ten!" everyone shouts. Except me.

"Henry. Are you following directions?"

"Yes, Teacher." And I show her.

"Henry, are you hungry AGAIN?"

"Not anymore," I reply.

burp

During lunch, I eat my fries first.

"Does anyone want to trade some fries for my broccoli?" I ask.

Addison does. Addison likes green things. I like his fries.

Parker says, "Too many fries aren't good for one's health, Henry."

I tell him they are great for mine, so he gives me some of his, too, and I stuff them in my pocket.

time!

I run out of time to eat my ham sandwich and apple and milk.

During gym class, Sir Tummy has more to say.

"Henry! **You're hungry** AGAIN!"

I ask to go to the bathroom, where I pull the last two smooshed fries from my pocket and eat them, along with a sticky lollipop from the Queen's Halloween stash.

My gym teacher, Mr. K., comes in to check on me. Thank goodness he doesn't know what I'm doing.

"Time to come back to gym, Henry," he says. "I don't want you to miss the quarter-mile run."

After just one lap around the gym, my legs are wobbling.

At the end of gym class, Mr. K. stands right beside me as he tells us one of his stay-fit stories.

Once there was a kingdom called Green Grub Valley. In this valley lived wizards who had special magical powers.

They could feed everyone in the kingdom—even the pig keeper and the rat catcher—from just one tiny garden. But one day, the candy troll and his thieves dug a long tunnel under the tiny garden, snatched away all the vegetables, and cast a sugar spell over the wizards.

Now the only things that grew in the garden were lollipops. At first, everyone loved it! But they grew weak and wobbly from eating only candy and couldn't even run at recess anymore. And since the wizards had lost their special planting powers, soon there was nothing growing in the tiny garden.

When word reached the castle, the king sent out his strongest knight, Sir Henry the Great. Riding in on his fiery dragon and shouting, "Sir Henry to the rescue!" the knight fed a magical sour pickle to each wizard to break the sugar spell.

Soon there were peas and cucumbers and all kinds of green things growing, and everyone, even the candy troll, ate better and stayed strong all year long.

THE END

When he finishes his story, Mr. K. looks right at me. "Class, any questions about how to eat better—and not **just** candy?"

Parker has one. "Mr. K., what is that room for?" He points to the door at the end of the gym.

"Oh, that's the teachers' lounge where teachers eat."

"Well," says Parker, "my sister Sophie says there are exercise machines in there for teachers. And that you guys have a fridge full of healthy stuff—like bean sprouts and nuts and probably broccoli. I bet that's how you teachers keep **your** special powers so you can teach us all year long."

Mr. K. smiles and says, "Parker, your sister is a smart girl."

Before school is out, Addison hands out his birthday treat. When he comes to me, I think of Mr. K.'s story.

"No thank you, Addison."

I'll wait until I get home to eat something, like maybe broccoli.

I play kickball after school while I wait for my mom to pick me up. Addison, the strongest boy in school, kicks a whopper, and it flies to the other side of the gym, knocking open the teachers' lounge door.

Parker and I
race to the door
to get our ball back.

We stop,
    we stare,

and we wonder
where Sophie gets
her information.

I grab our ball and
run away, hollering,
"Sir Henry to the
rescue!"

Teachers'
Lounge

When I get home, I make my rescue plan. I need to save the teachers and my family—even Her Highness—from growing weak from eating too much junk food!

I get up really early the next morning to carry out my plan. I promise the Queen I'll build her a throne if she helps me.

Together, we make breakfast for the whole kingdom—well, I mean my family.

Mom says, "Henry, this is the best breakfast ever! And these pickles— where on earth did you get this idea?"

After breakfast, Dad drives me to school. I've made sure we get there early for a change, so I can carry out the rest of my rescue plan.

I make my deliveries. I hope my teachers eat the healthy stuff I brought them. I don't want THEM to lose their special powers.

Kids like me are gonna need them all year long!

As for next year's Halloween, I already know what my costume will be.